The Singing Giant

Margaret Ryan
Illustrated by Jonathan Langley

 Rigby

George the Giant loved to sing.

He sang in the morning.

He sang in the evening.

He even sang
in the bathtub.

But some people in the village didn't like his singing.

"Stop that singing!" they said.

But George went on singing and singing and singing.

3

The people held a meeting.

"George must stop singing,"
said the moms and dads.
"He wakes us up at night."

"George must stop singing,"
said the grandmas and grandpas.
"He wakes us up in the morning."

"George must stop singing,"
said the sisters and brothers.
"We can't hear the television."

They went to see George.

George was singing in his garden.

"Have you come to hear me sing?" he asked.

"No, we can hear you all over the village.

Your singing must stop," said the people.

"But I love to sing," said George,
and a giant tear rolled down his cheek.
"You must stop singing," said the people.

George stopped singing.

"Now we'll be able
to sleep at night,"
said the moms and dads.

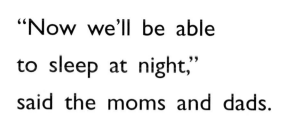

"Now we'll be able
to sleep in the morning,"
said the grandmas and grandpas.

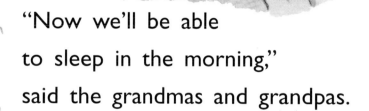

"Now we'll be able
to hear the television,"
said the sisters and brothers.

But the babies wouldn't go to sleep.

They cried in the morning.

They cried in the evening.

They even cried
in the bathtub.

"Please stop crying, and go to sleep,"
said everyone.

But the babies cried
          and cried
          and cried.

The moms and dads rocked the babies,
but they cried and cried and cried.

The grandmas and grandpas
took the babies for walks,
but they cried and cried and cried.

The sisters and brothers
played with the babies,
but they cried and cried and cried.

Then one little girl said,

"The babies didn't cry

when George was singing."

"You're right," said everyone.

"George must start singing again!"

They went to see George in his garden.

"Please start singing again," said the people.

"Then the babies will stop crying

and go to sleep.

They love your singing.

We're sorry we asked you to stop."

George the Giant smiled.
Then he started singing softly,
and the babies went to sleep.